ABRAHAM'S DREAM

WRITTEN AND ILLUSTRATED BY
EILEEN M. FOTI

To order additional copies of this book, contact:
Xlibris
844-714-8691
www.Xlibris.com
Orders@Xlibris.com

ISBN: 978-1-6698-5627-6 (sc)
ISBN: 978-1-6698-5628-3 (hc)
ISBN: 978-1-6698-5626-9 (e)

Print information available on the last page

Rev. date: 02/10/2023

DEDICATION

I WOULD LIKE TO THANK MY GRANDDAUGHTER, MIA WONG AND MY GOOD FRIEND, DEYSI UMANA FOR THEIR HELP IN RESEARCHING THIS BOOK. THEIR HELP IS APPRECIATED!

ON THE PAGES FACING THE ANIMAL DRAWINGS, I HAVE DRAWN THE TRACKS OF THE ANIMAL AND SOME OF THE FOODS THEY EAT. FOLLOWING IS A LIST OF THESE FOODS:

HORSE
PAGE 3 – CARROTS, GRASS, APPLE, OATS

BUNNY
PAGE 5 – CLOVER, APPLES, CARROTS, FLOWERS, GRASS

CHIPMUNK
PAGE 7 – ACORNS, NUTS AND BERRIES

TIGER
PAGE 9 - WILD PIG, FISH, LANGUR, PEAFOWL

RACCOON
PAGE 11 – FROGS, CORNS AND CLAMS

CAMEL
PAGE 13 – THORNY SHRUBS, DATES, TWIGS AND BEANS

KANGAROO
PAGE 15 – GRASS, FLOWERS

ELEPHANT
PAGE 17 - ACACIA, GRASSES, LEAVES

FOX
PAGE 19 – BERRIES, FISH, RABBITS AND EGGS

LION
PAGE 21 – ZEBRA, BABOON, REEDBUCK AND GIRAFFE

ABRAHAM WAS VERY SLEEPY. HE SPENT
MOST OF THE DAY AT THE ZOO, THERE
WERE SO MANY ANIMALS TO SEE.

EACH ANIMAL WAS DIFFERENT AND ABRAHAM
WANTED TO SEE THEM ALL. HE WALKED FROM CAGE
TO CAGE AND LISTENED WHILE HIS FATHER READ THE
SIGNS NEAR EACH CAGE, TELLING THE FACTS ABOUT
THE ANIMALS. HE DID NOT WANT TO LEAVE THE
ZOO, BUT HIS FATHER SAID IT WAS GETTING LATE
AND THEY WOULD NEED TO RETURN ANOTHER DAY.

THAT NIGHT, ABRAHAM LAY IN BED HE
THOUGHT ABOUT THE ANIMALS.

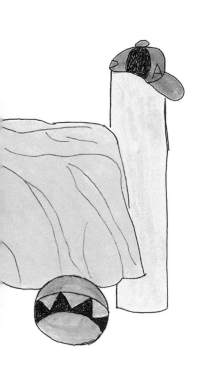

ALL AT ONCE ABRAHAM WAS A GALLOPING
HORSE. HEAD REARING BACK, MANE AND TAIL
FLYING IN THE WIND. ON HE RAN THROUGH
THE GREEN AND YELLOW GRASS OF THE
PLAINS. HIS EYES WERE STILL BROWN, BUT
NOW HE HAD FOUR LEGS INSTEAD OF TWO.

3

THE NEXT MINUTE ABRAHAM'S DREAM
CHANGED. HE IMAGINED HE WAS A
BUNNY SITTING QUIETLY IN THE GRASS
NIBBLING GIANT CLOVER LEAVES AND
FLOWERS. ABRAHAM HAS SEEN MANY
BUNNIES IN THE WOODS AND ON HIS
NEIGHBOR'S LAWNS AND NOW HE TOO
WAS A BUNNY. HE HAD TWO LONG EARS,
FLUFFY TAIL AND A PINK WIGGLY NOSE.

ALL OF A SUDDEN ABRAHAM'S
EARS SHRUNK. THEY BECAME SHORT
AND CLOSE TO HIS HEAD. IN HIS
WOODLAND HOME HE WAS NOW
EATING ACORNS, FROM THE LARGE
OAK TREE, BERRIES AND NUTS.
ABRAHAM WAS A CHIPMUNK. HIS
CHEEK POUCHES WERE FULL AND
HIS FACE LOOKED PUFFY. A WHITE
STRIPE GOING DOWN HIS BACK
LED TO A STRAIGHT LITTLE TAIL.

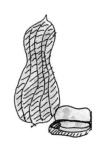

ABRAHAM THEN TURNED INTO A
STALKING TIGER THROUGH THE GRASS,
PEERING BETWEEN THE OPENINGS OF
LARGE LEAVES GROWING ON PLANTS
COVERING THE JUNGLE FLOOR. HE
HAD LONG WHISKERS AND BEAUTIFUL
BLACK STRIPES, WHICH HELPED HIM
TO HIDE AMONG THE PLANTS IN
THE JUNGLE. HE FELT SO STRONG AS
HE PROWLED THROUGH THE GRASS
STRETCHING HIS FOUR POWERFUL LEGS.

ABRAHAM'S MOTHER ALWAYS TOLD HIM
TO WASH HIS HANDS BEFORE HE ATE SO
NOW NOT ONLY WAS HE WASHING HIS
HANDS, BUT HE WAS ALSO WASHING HIS
FOOD! HE WAS A GOOD RACCOON AND
WAS DOING WHAT ALL RACCOONS DO.
ON HIS FACE, HE WORE A MASK AND ON
HIS LONG BUSHY TAIL HE WORE RINGS OF
COLOR. HE LOOKED LIKE A LITTLE BANDIT
AS HE WALKED AROUND HIS FOREST HOME.

THE FOREST WAS NICE AND COOL AND
ABRAHAM LIKED THE SMELL OF THE TREES.
ABRAHAM TURNED OVER IN BED AND NOW
THE FOREST CHANGED AND HE STOOD IN
THE HOT SANDY DESERT, UNDER THE BRIGHT
SUN. HE WAS NOW A CAMEL WITH A LARGE
HUMP ON HIS BACK. HIS EARS WERE STILL
SMALL BUT HIS NECK GREW QUITE LONG.
HARD DATES, TWIGS AND THORNY SHRUBS
WERE NOW HIS FAVORITE FOODS. CAMELS
DO NOT NEED A LOT OF WATER TO SURVIVE
IN THE DESERT SO ABRAHAM DID NOT
HAVE TO GET UP FOR A DRINK DURING THE
NIGHT AND THEREFORE, HE COULD STAY
IN BED AND ENJOY BEING A CAMEL.

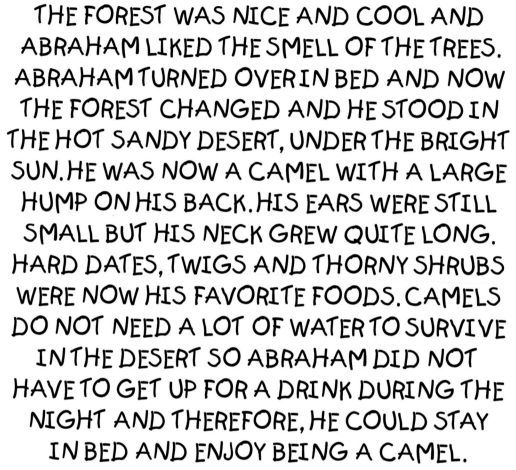

ABRAHAM STARTED TO HOP. THEN HE
REALIZED HE HAD TURNED INTO A
KANGAROO. PLAYFULLY, HE HOPPED
AMONG THE OTHER KANGAROOS. SOME
OF THE KANGAROOS CARRIED BABIES,
CALLED JOEY'S IN THEIR POUCHES.
ABRAHAM THOUGHT IT WOULD BE
GREAT IF HIS MOM HAD A POUCH.

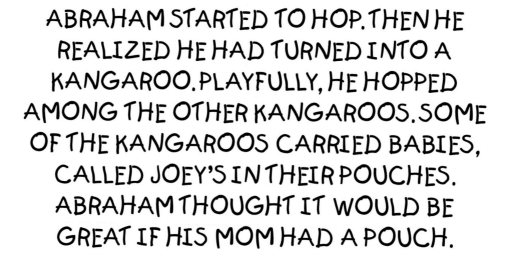

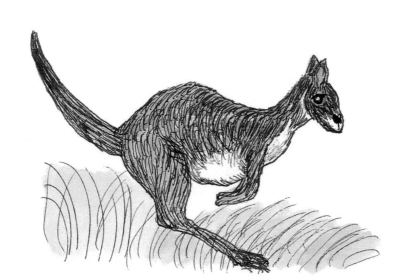

ABRAHAM HEARD A TRUMPETING NOISE.
THEN HE REALIZED HE HAD MADE THIS
NOISE BECAUSE NOW HE WAS AN ELEPHANT!
AS AN ELEPHANT, ABRAHAM WAS QUITE
LARGE. ALTHOUGH HIS FEET WERE WIDE,
TO SUPPORT HIS WEIGHT, HE DID NOT
LEAVE MANY TRACKS WHEN HE WALKED
THROUGH THE FOREST. HIS HIND FEET
STEPPED INTO THE TRACKS OF HIS FRONT
FEET. HE HAD TUSKS, VERY LARGE EARS
AND A LONG TRUNK, WITH HIS TRUNK HE
COULD DRINK WATER AND PULL BRANCHES
DOWN, FROM TALL TREES TO EAT LEAVES.

SUDDENLY ABRAHAM HAD A BUSHY
RED TAIL, TWO LARGE EARS, SHREWD
EYES AND NOW HE HAD TURNED INTO
A RED FOX. AS A FOX, ABRAHAM
LIVED IN THE WOODS AND ENJOYED
EATING, JUICY RED BERRIES.

AS ABRAHAM WAS ENJOYING BEING A FOX, A LOUD ROAR RANG OUT. HE NOTICED HE HAD WHISKERS AND A LONG MANE, FOUR LEGS WITH LARGE PAWS AND A TAIL. ABRAHAM WAS A LION! HE FELT STRONG AND PROUD AS HE WALKED AROUND WITH OTHER LIONS. A LARGE LION WAS WALKING TOWARD HIM. THE LION WAS GROWLING AND LOOKING MEAN. SUDDENLY HE JUMPED AT ABRAHAM. ABRAHAM FELT THE LION'S WET TONGUE ON HIS FACE. ABRAHAM SCREAMED.

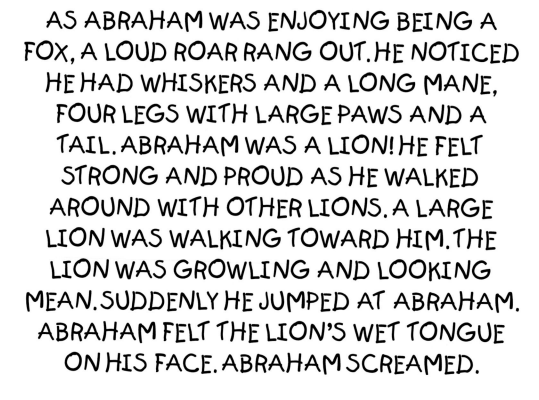

ABRAHAM AWOKE TO FIND HIS TABBY CAT LICKING
HIS CHEEK. AT FIRST, HIS TABBY CAT LOOKED
AS A LARGE AS A LION BUT WHEN ABRAHAM
WAS FULLY AWAKE, HE REALIZED HIS TABBY CAT
WAS SMALL AND CUTE AND VERY GENTLE.

ABRAHAM WAS HAPPY TO BE SAFE AT HOME.
HOWEVER VISITING THE ZOO, HAD BEEN A
GREAT ADVENTURE AND HE WAS EAGER TO GO TO
SCHOOL TO TELL HIS FRIENDS ALL ABOUT IT!

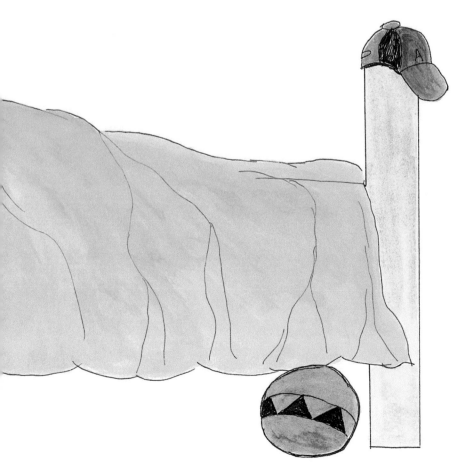

Printed in the United States
by Baker & Taylor Publisher Services